Winter Wishes

by Apple Jordan

illustrated by Elisa Marrucchi

Random House 🏠 New York

Winter is here!

Chilly winds blow.

The outside sparkles.

There is so much snow.

It is a frosty season.

There is a lot to do.

It is the time of year

when wishes come true.

Outside is coated
with fluffy snow.
Inside, Snow White
pours cups of cocoa.

She trims the tree
with stars and bells.

She fills the cottage
with warm cookie smells.

She makes a wish
on a star so bright.

Then the Dwarfs
sing and dance
into the night.

Ariel wishes
for a wintry bash.

A holiday parade
makes a big splash!

The jolly friends
dance around the tree.
Winter is fun
under the sea.

Lovely Belle wishes
for a big winter feast.
Mrs. Potts makes one
for her and the Beast.

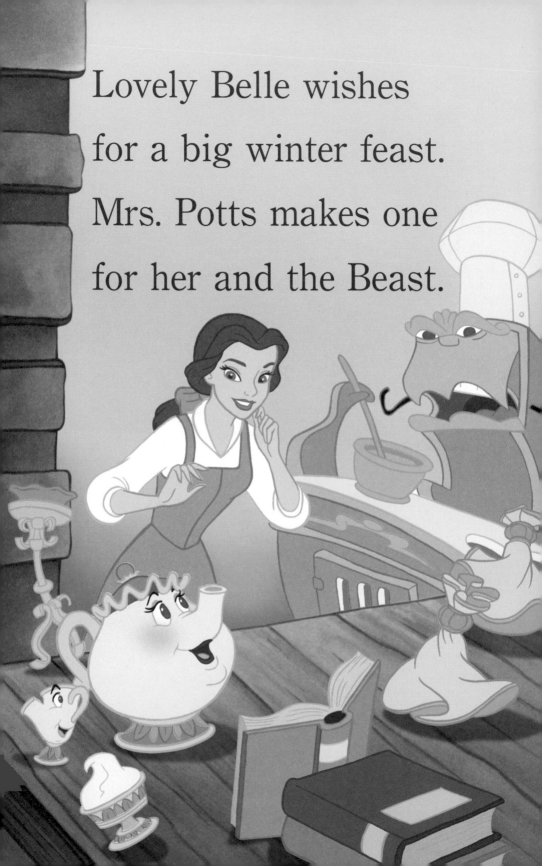

The meal is served
and piled up high.
Roast turkey, cider,
and warm apple pie!

Everyone shares
in the holiday cheer.

It is such a joy
to have friends so dear.

Briar Rose sings
a wishful love song.
A snowbird sweetly
chirps right along.

21

Sing, strum,
hum, tweet!
A winter concert
never sounded
so sweet.

Jasmine wishes to see
a world with snow . . .

24

. . . and a snowman
dressed in a hat
and a bow!

Abracadabra!
Alakazoo!
Genie makes her
wish come true.

26

Cinderella wishes to go
on a snowy coach ride.
So Prince Charming
takes his lovely bride.

The coach brings them
to a grand winter ball.

Then they happily dance
in the snowfall.

Make a winter wish.

It is fun to do.

You never know when

the dream may come true.